It was Polly's birthday.
Sal and Polly went to
Cloud Nine.

"Wow!" said Polly.

"What shall we do first?"

espresso
education

Phonics

Cloud
Nine

Gill Budgell

W

First published in 2012 by
Franklin Watts
338 Euston Road
London NW1 3BH

Franklin Watts Australia
Level 17/207 Kent Street
Sydney NSW 2000

Text and illustration © Franklin Watts 2012

The Espresso characters are originated and
designed by Claire Underwood and Pesky Ltd.

The Espresso characters are the property of
Espresso Education Ltd.

A CIP catalogue record for this book is
available from the British Library.

ISBN: 978 1 4451 0748 6 (hbk)
ISBN: 978 1 4451 07516 (pbk)

Illustrations by Artful Doodlers Ltd.
Art Director: Jonathan Hair
Series Editor: Jackie Hamley
Project Manager: Gill Budgell
Series Designer: Matthew Lilly

Printed in China

Franklin Watts is a division of
Hachette Children's Books,
an Hachette UK company.

www.hachette.co.uk

Level 1 50 words
Concentrating on CVC words plus and, the, to

Level 2 70 words
Concentrating on double letter sounds and new letter
sounds (ck, ff, ll, ss, j, v, w, x, y, z, zz) plus no, go, I

Level 3 100 words
Concentrating on new graphemes (qu, ch, sh, th, ng,
ai, ee, igh, oa, oo, ar, or, ur, ow, oi, ear, air, ure, er)
plus he, she, we, me, be, was, my, you, they, her, all

Level 4 150 words
Concentrating on adjacent consonants (CVCC/CCVC
words) plus said, so, have, like, some, come, were, there,
little, one, do, when, out, what

Level 5 180 words
Concentrating on new graphemes (ay, wh, ue, ir, ou, aw,
ph, ew, ea, a-e, e-e, i-e, o-e, u-e) plus day, very, put, time,
about, saw, here, came, made, don't, asked, looked,
called, Mrs

Level 6 200 words
Concentrating on alternative pronunciations (c, ow, o, g, y)
and spellings (ee, ur, ay, or, m, n, air, l, r) plus your, don't
time, saw, here, very, make, their, called, asked, looked

"I like the dolphins,"
said Sal.

So they swam with the dolphins.

"I like the elephants," said Polly.

So they had an
elephant ride!

Next they saw the
big roundabout.

They went round
and round.
They went in
and out.

Next they found the Slide
and Glide.

"Look at that girl," said Sal.
"She will slide down and splash."

They took a photo.

"Why don't we go in Bird
Mountain?" said Polly.
They held hands
and crept inside ...

Squawk!

"What was that sound?"
asked Sal.

Then they saw a big bird!
It thrust a sharp claw
at them.
"Let's get out!" said Sal.

They were glad
to be out of
Bird Mountain.

Sal said, "It's time for a nice rest."

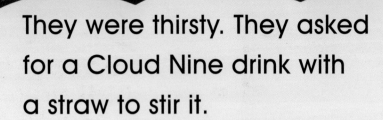

They were thirsty. They asked for a Cloud Nine drink with a straw to stir it.

Polly got a Cloud Nine birthday bag ...

Puzzle Time

Find the six sound pairs!

One has been done for you.

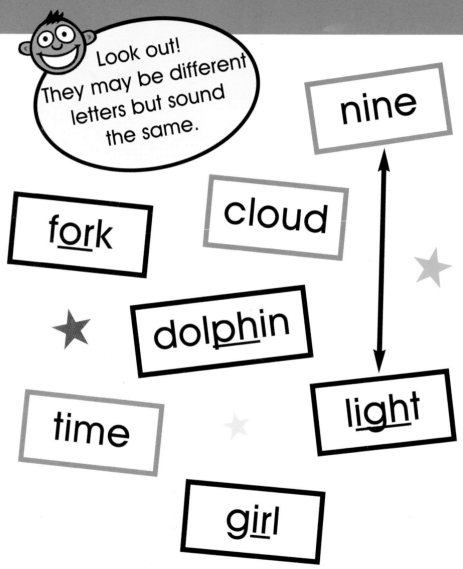

Look out! They may be different letters but sound the same.

nine

cloud

f<u>or</u>k

dol<u>ph</u>in

time

li<u>gh</u>t

g<u>ir</u>l

saw

photo

<u>ow</u>l

purse

n<u>igh</u>t

Answers

nine – light is already completed to show you the first pair.

time/nine – both /igh/
girl/purse – both /ur/
cloud/owl – both /ow/

saw/fork – both /or/
dolphin/photo – both /f/

A note about the phonics in this book

Concentrating on new phonemes
In this book children practise reading new graphemes (letters) for some
phonemes (sounds) that they already know. For example, they already know
that the letters igh make the /igh/ sound but now they are practising that i-e can
also make the /igh/ sound.

Known phoneme	New graphemes	Words in the story
/igh/	i-e	nine, ride, slide, glide, like, inside, time, nice
/ur/	ir	birthday, first, girl, bird, thirsty, stir
/ow/	ou	cloud, roundabout, round, out, found, mountain, sound
/or/	aw	saw, claw, squawk, straw
/f/	ph	dolphins, elephant(s), photo
common words	time, saw, don't, (birth)day	
tricky common words	asked	

Remind the children about the letters they already know for these phonemes.

In the puzzle they are challenged to match the words that have the same
sound in them; same sound but different letters.

Top tip: if a child gets stuck on a word then ask them to try and sound it out and
then blend it together again or show them how to do this. For example,
birthday, b-ir-th-d-ay, birthday.